Winston
and
Mira

Joan C Mullins

To order additional copies of this book, contact:
Xlibris
844-714-8691
www.Xlibris.com
Orders@Xlibris.com

ISBN: Softcover   978-1-6698-3818-0
         EBook   978-1-6698-3819-7

Print information available on the last page

Rev. date: 08/22/2022

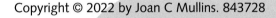

Stories by Joan C Mullins

Home With Winston
And Mira

From the very day I picked these two adorable puppies up at the airport the Love was immediate.

They had gotten lost at the airport... it was a terrible wait for them to be found. The airport had not taken them to the proper pick up area.

Finally, the attendant appeared. He apologized for the mix up as he handed the kennel to me... Thank goodness they did not die on the flight from Oklahoma.

My son Tommy was with me. He said Mom I will drive us home, the airport was located in Charleston and he knew how excited I was.

Tommy said... sit in the back with them and get to know them... These two beautiful little faces looked up at me. Oh... these poor little puppies just did not know what was going on. .

The trip home felt like hours...Turning into Sun City... my home was only two blocks away...

I could not wait to take them out of the kennel. It had been a long journey for them and I just wanted to hold them... hug and kiss these two beautiful babies that were finally home with me.

As I took them out of there kennel they started sniffing around... of course these pups had no idea where they were.

I let them smell there new surroundings and then I introduced them to the backyard where they will go to use as there potty.

The next few weeks they became part of the household.

They were smart little puppies and they caught right on about doing potty outside.

Maybe a little accident every now and then. I did not scold them just took them outside right away.

They had many toys to play with and bones to chew on.

The bones were OK to give them...specifically they were eatable for eating without a problem.

So daily after they ate there chicken... these safe chewy bones as I called them were given as a treat.

They both guarded them... bringing them to there beds and lay with them before they devoured them... which took many hours.

They both would leave a little piece of the bone...

During the day they would keep this small pieces in there mouth while they walked around and both would growl at each other if they tried to take it

Needless to say... I would take these small pieces away from them as they would drop them...both of them looking at me saying hey "mom" why did you do that.?

I knew puppies love to chew on things that they should not... a few times I caught them trying to bite my bookcase leg. I then would say "no" "no" and then I would give them a toy of there's.

They were very smart and they listened to me.

I needed to make an appointment to see the vet... although they already had some shots I knew that they needed more to keep them in good health

All was looking great so the needed shots were given. "hurrah" they both were in good condition.

Now another new journey for all of us had started.

When night came I would put them into the kennel... The kennel was large and they fit into it with comfort.

The nights and day's came and went. It was now time that I decided to let them roam the house after hours.

They were so smart as I keep saying and I was so happy that they were wonderful pups.

I made sure that I had beds for them in different rooms... They had a choice to go where they wanted to sleep.

Another journey was to take place also.

My son Tommy had a beautiful mixed large dog...he weighed almost 100 pounds.

Tommy named him Rocky...because... at one time Tommy was going through some rough times and Rocky was his Savior. He helped Tommy get through those terrible day's

Tommy had moved to South Carolina to be close to me.

A nice Town House was found for Tommy and Rocky only a few miles from me.

He would bring Rocky for visits often and the pups got use to being around this large animal...the pups would get up into his mouth and he gently would lick them.

Winston and Mira loved when Tommy would appear... It was happy days for all of us.

Tommy loved them so much and he was glad to take them for a walk down the street.

This area was where neighbors would take there dogs for a walk also.

Winston and Mira were so funny to watch... As the day's went on they enjoyed barking... it was the outstanding fun for the day. And in between a nap was a definite for them.

Fun of course was hiding there goodies in different places so each one of them could not find them...this was a blast... as they would go around smelling there beds and scratching at the small scatter rugs that were around .

Some times they would forget where they put them as I would find one or two under a chair or my bed.

Everyday they would run from the front door to the back door especially when the ground keepers came to mow the grass and to blow the debris that was around the yard.

The wonderful years came and went but not before there little bodies had health issues.

They both had bladder stones and of course this so hurtful for them as they had to have few surgeries to take them out.

Winston had pancreas troubles. He would have bloody bowels alerting me that he was having this issue.

He would have to stay at the vet's for a few day's while they injected medicines. Thank God... The vet took care of him.

After his stay at the vet's his diet was changed that he would have to stay on a low fat diet.

So I ordered the special food for him and of course little Mira had to endure this diet also for her sake.

It was very hard on them... they lost weight as the food really did not have a flavor.

It broke my heart to see this... After a few years I decided to take charge of my babies. I checked around about diets for dogs.

Then I read many stories of what I could feed them without fear of hurting there bodies.

I found dog foods that were lower in fat. Then I started giving them fresh chicken breasts by boiling them and incorporating them with the regular dry soft dog food I had found.

Also, they love cooked carrots.

Both of the pups did not like eating there food from a bowl... They liked to eat off of the floor. How horrid this was. I researched about this strange happening and found many dogs liked to eat that way.

I was upset of course so... I looked on line and found dog mats... I never thought about mats for dogs.

So I ordered them... They are small heavy square mats with little pickies all over the middle of the square.

The story of why this is so is because dogs like to feel these little pickies on there tongue so they say. True...as Winston and Mira never ate off the floor again.

Amazing to me was that this diet gave them what they liked and there lives turned around and they put weight on.

I did talk with the Vet telling him what I decided to do and of course he was not really happy about this. I said I do understand what you are telling me Thank you.

They have stayed pretty healthy...Until...

I took them to the vet's when I was asked to...they proceeded to take the x-rays... making sure they were doing well.

Sadly an x-ray showed that Mira had a mass on her lung.

It was not cancer... The years have gone by and she has not had any issues with this mass. It was growing very slowly. Not to worry the vet said.

Over the years I have been so grateful that I have them in my life. Having them around me daily with there silly antics has given me a reason to get up every morning.

They have bought me Joy and Sadness... This is what life is all about.

This is the year 2020 and they will be 12 years old this May.

I thank God that I have been so lucky to have them in my life.

Sadly in 2021 Mira's mass became cancer. The cancer grew so fast that I had to put her to sleep.

I miss her dearly every day.

Winston also lost his friend and he did not bark for two months after Mira passed.

It is now 2022 and Winston doing very well no problems at this time.

Of course I will be devastated when I will need to let Winston go.

Winston and Mira

MIRA

WINSTON

WINSTON

MIRA

WINSTON   MIRA

Jacks
Traveling
Turtles

Winston and Mira had made friends with two American Box Turtles from the Missouri Ozark's.

"King Kush" is a 15-year-old, fully grown male and little "Sativa" is a small but growing female of nearly years. She fits snugly into a soup ladle.

Both turtles belong to my friends Jack. They are known as "Jacks Two Travelling Turtles" Jack takes them everywhere he goes- including airplanes trips stowed in a "turtle tote!"

Every time Jack visits me, Winston and Mira have a blast playing with them.

They bark when the turtles crawl under the pups sleeping bed. Mira exhausts herself scratching crazily at her mysterious moving bed as the turtles slowly drag the beds across the floor.

It's pure comedy and we laugh so hard as the dogs try to uncover the culprits!

After the dogs are exhausted, we put the turtles on my enclosed patio to eat and drink. After feasting, the turtles seek out a nice quiet corner of the patio for a long nights sleep.

Pets In My Life

After the sadness of my kitten time passed. We bought a dog. She was so beautiful, we named her Gypsy.
More sadness, my mom and dad divorced. We had to leave our home as it was put on the market for sale.

Mom found different apartments where we lived. Finally one was found, it had three rooms, and a bathroom. Poor Gypsy had to be locked in the bath-room because my brother and I went to school and mom had to work.

This beautiful animal had to stay in that room until one of us got home to let her out. How cruel this was and I could not do anything about this situation.

The day came when we had to give her up. She was ill, my heart sickened. I loved her so much.

I never had another animal for many years.

Getting married and having children pets were introduced. Fishes, hamsters and lizards.

Not to be-forgotten, dogs.

Once in awhile my husband would bring home a stray. But this did not work out for the family. They usually were ill animals and we had to take them to the pound.

One birthday I was surprised with this adorable black puppy. A little girl. I named her Jingles as it was just before the holidays.

I had my Jingles or 12 years. She became ill and I had to put her to sleep. How horrid it was.

She, somehow knew it was the end for her. She kept staring at me and my husband.

My Dear little Jingles then gave a little flap of her tail to say good-by. And she was gone.

A few months passed. Then one day as I was shopping at the mall I saw a gal offering puppies for sale.

Naturally, I stopped and spoke about the puppies. These little ones were only 6 weeks and not old enough to bring home.

I would have to wait another 2 weeks before they were able to leave there mom.

I told the gal I was interested in getting one so she said I had a pick of the litter as I was the first person inquiring about them. I then choose the first born. A girl

The breed: "Schnauzer."

Finally the day came that I would be able to take this little puppy home with me.

There she was so cute.

Picking her up I gently kissed and hugged her.

Her body coat was gray and white and the hair was wavy.

I named her Ashley.

During this time my son Tommy found a little puppy on the road. He told me some guy in a truck w trying to run her down.

Seeing this he stopped his car and picked up this little black body.

Tommy was on his way to work so he took the puppy with him.

When I got to work Tommy said Mom look what I found on the road. Tommy had laid this little puppy on an old carpet, he was all curled up and shaking.

I called the vet. And told about this little pup and the vets office said bring him in right away.

The vet took him in his arms and checked him over, then holding him by the scuff of his neck he started spraying him with a chemical. He was infested with fleas. The vet said the fleas were eating him up.

He then gave him all the vaccinations the he needed

Tommy took him home, but after about 6 months he felt so sorry that he had to leave him alone all day so he asked me to take care of him so-therefore he lived with me until his death at 14 years old.

Ashley became ill before Bullit. She passed on.

"Bullit" was his name for his little body trying to stay away from cars trying to kill him. Tommy was his savior.

After the sadness of losing my dear pets once again. It was around six months later.

I found a little brown-orange haired Yorkie. He was in pet shop that was located at mall in Florida

He had been named Pumpkin, and I kept this name. I loved this little guy, he was a good pup. He was 7 years old when he became ill.

The vet could no save him as he had lost all but 10% of his kidney's.

Once again I had to face sadness. I had him cremated also and placed his ashes next to my other dear pups.

This time 3 month s passed. I got lonesome...Of course! I wanted to get another dog.

It did not take long as I got on-line and found a breeder of Yorkie's. .

Within a few weeks and looking at pictures of Yorkie's I picked the last of a litter a little boy, and then I picked a little girl from the same breeder but a different mom.

The home for the e pups were in another state, I now had to fly them to me. Anxiously waiting for the day they would arrive at the airport, and praying they would be in good condition from there journey.

I arrived at the airport earlier then the plane landing.

A scare came when they told me they could not find them after the plane landed.

After an hour or so the airport attendant comes walking down the ramp holding a crate with these 2 adorable Yorkie's.

Quickly, I gave them a quick exam. Both of them were in great condition from that long journey.

I could not wait until I got home.

This was now to be another journey in my life as well as theirs

I named them:

"Winston a d Mira"

The pups were easy to train. They were loving to everybody

Going outside potty was a feat for them as they were tiny and the grass almost covered them.

I crated them for a short time They did not like being in a crate.

I decided to take a chance giving them the run of the home.

They were the best "babies." as I called them.

WINSTON

ROCKY

TOMMY (SON)

BULLIT AND ASHLEY

PUMPKIN

JOAN HOLDING PUMPKIN

There Is Always A Beginning

I grew up in a wonderful Christian family. I loved attending church. Remembering that I had to wait until I was old enough to receive the host of Jesus.

My mom bought a beautiful piano and took lesson with a woman whose name was Miss Hurt.

The time came when my brother and I were to take lesson also. I did not fare well with the lessons and I complained she was a Ms. Hurt teacher... Mom was disappointment. The reality was I just did not want to take lessons... I rather have a pet.

I wanted to have a doll carriage and a pet to put in it. Finally one Christmas I received my request and within a few days I got a pet. An adorable kitty.

So much fun I had dressing it and taking it for walks. One weekend I was taken to my Grandmothers for a weekend visit. Mom told my she would take care of the kitty. But it ended in a disaster as this man that lived across from us did not like animals and he would put poison food out to keep the animals away. Sadly Mom had let the kitty out and she got into the poison and died. My first pet gone.

Many months went by...Mom agreed that we could have another pet... I really do not remember how this adorable dog came into our family but she was accepted and her name would be named Gypsy.

Time passed and my beautiful family life ended as my Mom and Dad got divorced. Mom sold the house and we ended living in a terrible 3 room apartment with Gypsy. It was terrible as we had to leave Gypsy in the closed bathroom as Mom had to work and my brother and I had to attend school. Gypsy did not fare well of course and this one day my brother unknown to me took her to the pound...How sad, but I could not do anything about it.

Years passed I married, having four children...During my son who lived near by and was was working with his dad in the shop...

One morning Tommy going to work rescued a puppy trying to cross a busy highway.

A lovely black little guy, he was so much fun to be around and he was named Bullit ...after awhile it was difficult for Tommy to get home during the day to let Bullit out and he asked me if I would take him as I had a large backyard. Gladly... he became my pet... and a big part of my life.

One day I decided to get another puppy because when I was at a Mall I saw puppies for sale. That's all

I had to see. Sooooo

I bought a darling gray hair in color puppy... I named her Ashley, Bulllit and she got along immediately

About the Author

Joan C Mullins was born in Jersey City, New Jersey. Moving to South Carolina many years later, she retired to peruse her hobby of painting and venture into writing children's stories. For a time, Joan's stories were tucked away in a dark corner of a closet. Finding them and reading them all over again gave her chuckles, as they had, once before.

"The Mystical Garden"
"The Frog and The Bee"
"The Butterfly"
"The Cemetery"
"The Drum"
"Intergalactic Surprise"
"The Cow and the Nanny Goat" (A new addition to her children's books)

In the year 2010, two of the stories, "The Mystical Garden," and the "Frog and The Bee", were produced as a Ballet. This production of the Ballet was presented on Hilton Head Island, South Carolina. Two hundred children danced in this two-day event that was also filmed. Joan also penned her story "Reflections". Her words of family and life. Unbelievably, on November 19, 2010, Joan's son, Tommy, was brutality murdered. Joan wrote about his murder. Her book is called "The Ending".

Printed in the United States
by Baker & Taylor Publisher Services